Ir

In Plain Sight

For more information go to fionarosefisher.com

To all young authors, the world needs your work.

-FF

Author's note: The events of this story took place between 1986 and 1990. An account was found in the rubble of a house destroyed by The Great Flood of 1993. I decided that the account's story needed to be told. After extensive research, the account transformed into this story. According to police and historical records of the time, the people are real and the events are accurate. To protect the identity of the people mentioned, I will not reveal the location of this girl's journey.

Prologue

"Anna, I have something to tell you," Ms. Melvins said.

"Okay," Anna looked up from her book and waited for whatever Ms. Melvins had to tell her.

Ms. Melvins looked at the other girls. "Alone," she clarified.

"Um, okay." Anna got up and nervously followed Ms. Melvins out of the room and into her office. Ms. Melvins never had to tell the girls something in private unless they were adopted. Was that what had happened? Had Anna finally been adopted?

"This note was tucked in your blankets when you were dropped off at the orphanage," Ms. Melvins explained as she pulled a piece of paper out of her pocket. "I decided not to give it to you until you were older."

Anna was crushed. She had been hoping for a new family, someone to love her, and all she got was a remnant of her old family, the one that had given her up eleven years ago. She sighed and grabbed the note from Ms. Melvins.

Anna read the note twice and then a third time. It was worded strangely and every sentence was a new paragraph. Could her parents be trying to tell her something? Were they trying to spell out F...O...R...E...S...T?

One

Anna set down the book she had been reading and sighed.

"Wow guys! I think we just witnessed a miracle! Anna can't concentrate on her book," Lizzie exclaimed and smirked at Anna. She was always giving Anna a hard time about how much she read.

"Oh, be quiet Lizzie," Charlene scolded.

"She's just mad that you got higher grades than her first semester," Laura said reassuringly, but Anna wasn't happy. *Yes, but higher grades aren't going to get me a proper home and family,* Anna thought to herself.

Almost as if she had guessed what Anna was thinking, Charlene hugged Anna, "Remember we're all family here."

"But you guys don't understand. Most of you knew your parents before you were sent here. You knew that you had a family once. I don't," Anna tried hard not to pout. She knew right then that she had to make a choice, she could either sit in this orphanage for the rest of her life or take a risk and run away. It wasn't like thirteen year olds were getting adopted left and right. "Grades can wait! I have a much bigger journey ahead of me." She hadn't realized she said anything out loud until all the girls in the room gasped.

"What are you talking about? How can grades wait?" Charlene asked Anna curiously.

"I'm leaving," Anna announced. "I have to find my family." She started to pack up all of her belongings. It wasn't much, just some clothes, bedsheets, her books, a stack of report cards, a pocket knife, matches, her savings and her cat, Sheila, who had stuffed herself in her cat carrier. She grabbed the duffel bag and cat carrier and shuffled awkwardly out the door. *Well so much for a dramatic exit.*

Anna looked around the first floor. She didn't want to be caught by Ms. Melvins. If she did get caught, Anna then would be under Ms. Melvins' watchful eye for the next five years until Anna turned eighteen.

"Bye!" she heard Charlene yell. "Good luck. We'll miss you." Her voice broke at this and Anna saw her turn away from the window to hide her tears.

Anna had to respond to this, she might never see Charlene again, "I'll miss you, too!" She turned around and walked away, not looking back once, afraid that if she did, the tears beginning to blur her vision would start to flow down her cheeks.

Two

Beth was completely focused. She breathed in as she drew the curve of the lips and added a rosy red color to them. She breathed out and drew the gentle curve of a cheek. The face she was drawing was a chubby baby face, it had deep blue eyes and soft red cheeks.

Beth sighed and slipped the drawing onto a pile of papers. Every paper had the same face drawn over and over again with several different expressions. Beth had always been able to draw beautiful pictures, but she had never taken an interest in portraits until now. Even now all she drew was this face. It was like her brain was trying to make her remember something.

She jumped when she heard a knock on the door. She walked over to the door and opened it. Standing there was her parents' secretary. The secretary looked around at Beth's room, the walls were covered from top to bottom with drawings and posters to cover the white space. Beth hated plainness.

"Oh, are my parents going to be home late again?" Beth asked brightly, trying to hide her disappointment.

"No," the secretary said solemnly. "Beth, I'm afraid that your parents have gone missing."

"What? Accountants don't just 'go missing'!"

"Well, your parents did just 'go missing' and until they are found you will be living with your aunt. Here is some money for a train ticket and a suitcase," the secretary responded. "I will be here tomorrow morning to drop you off at the train station." She quickly closed the door and left. Beth's first thought was, *Who leaves a girl whose parents just went missing alone in a house for a night?* Her parents' secretary was usually a lot more responsible than this.

Where could her parents be? It *is* true that accountants don't go missing. Beth thought about it a bit more and decided that the secretary didn't need to pick her up. She was thirteen after all. Beth would be able to get to Aunt Ruth's house on her own. All she had to do was walk to the train, buy a ticket and ride to her aunt's house.

She hoped it was Aunt Ruth that she would be staying with because she ran an orphanage for girls and Beth could make some great friends while she stayed there. Beth hoped that it would not be her other aunt. Beth always felt afraid when her parents spoke about that aunt. There was something sinister about her that her parents never wanted to talk about. Not that they had much time to talk to Beth anyway.

So she packed her suitcase with some clothes, books and her savings. She picked up her dog, Mr. Fluffy Pants and headed towards the door. As she opened the door she noticed a rolled up piece of paper in the keyhole. Where had that come from? Had the secretary left it there? She unrolled it and immediately recognized her mother's handwriting.

Dearest Beth,
Even if we had to go, we will always come back.
Coming back will not be as easy as you think.
It is incredible how small of a world it is, and we will meet again soon.

Dogs protect you, so stay close to Mr. Fluffy Pants.
Under the grass and into the hole is where you will find us.

Often many things will try to keep people apart.
Unless you give up, you will find us.
Success will be yours.

Three

After leaving the orphanage, Anna really had no idea where to start. Her plan seemed so much simpler in her head. Figure out who her parents were, find them, live happily ever after, the end. Anna realized that it wasn't going to be that simple now. First she was going to have to find the orphanage's records of her parents. Where would you go to find the orphanage's records? Anna knew that Ms. Melvins kept them under lock and key, but she might be able to find them on the computer at the nearest library. She could buy a train ticket and ride to the nearest town with a library, but that would use up most of her savings.

There was no other solution, so she walked slowly to the train station. She wanted to savor this moment and remember it so when she found her family she could tell them over and over again how she had come home. *If* she ever found her family. She couldn't let that thought crush her. She inspected every little detail of the sidewalk and the forest nearby. She was so distracted that she ran into a girl who had been walking towards the train station.

"Hey!" the girl exclaimed.

"Sorry, Sorry," Anna apologized.

"That's okay. Where are you going?" asked the girl curiously.

"Well right now I'm going to the train station," Anna answered quickly. For some reason she felt like she shouldn't give away too much to this curious girl. She was thin and had sparking blue eyes. Anna thought the girl looked a bit like how she would imagine herself to look if she had a proper family to take care of her.

"So why are you getting on the train?" the girl asked. "My name is Beth by the way, what's yours?"

"My name is Anna and I'm getting on the train because I'm looking for my family. I haven't seen them since I was two," she answered quietly, hoping Beth would not make a big deal about her being an orphan.

"Oh, I'm sorry, I would be devastated if anything happened to my parents," Beth sympathized. "Well, actually something did happen to my parents." She suddenly remembered why she was on the train in the first place. "They disappeared just today, that's why I'm getting on the train. I have to live with my aunt until they are found."

Although Anna was sorry for Beth she had to ask, "So you're not going to do anything about it?"

"Well I thought I should just leave it to the authorities," Beth explained.

Anna was surprised. "The authorities have been searching for my parents for eleven years and they have found nothing! No sign, no clue, not even a birth certificate. All they left was this little note and if they were trying to tell me anything with it, it would be forest," she explained bitterly.

"What?" Beth asked.

Anna took out the note that Ms. Melvins had given her and showed it to Beth.

For my young girl, Anna Mayes.
Oh, we never wanted to let you go.
Rain will fall on our hearts when we think of you.
Every person has a purpose and you were meant to be without us, but only for a short time.
Such a small world this is that I hope we meet again one day.
Truly and always your mother.

"Okay," Beth said, "and why do you think that your mom is trying to tell you forest?"

"Read down the beginning letter of each line," Anna explained.

"Oh!" Beth said. "I see it. Wait!" She pulled her note out of her pocket.

"What if?" She read her mother's note, spelling out the first letter of each line, "D...E...C...I...D...U...O...U...S..." She sat there for a moment. "Wow, if that is a word, then it is amazing that both of our parents decided to leave us the same code."

"Well it does sound like it could be a word, but I'm not sure what it means. Maybe I will look it up when I go to the library."

"Can I come with you then?" Beth asked.

"Don't you have to go to your aunt's house?" Anna asked.

"But if my parents are trying to leave me a message I have to find out what it is! If we were together we would be able to help each other find our families," Beth exclaimed. "I can get a ticket to go with you instead of one going to my aunt's. I'm assuming you're going to head east." Beth pointed in the direction of the town that Anna was heading. "It is the only town with a library near here."

Anna was so taken back by Beth's friendliness that she was speechless for a moment as she thought over her deal. She was conflicted. Would she really be safe going off with a strange girl to search for their families? Was it all a trap? But she had to find her family! Finally she agreed.

"Great. Let's go get the tickets!" Beth said excitedly.

Anna wasn't sure about Beth, she seemed in a rush. She needed to slow down before she accidentally ran right off a cliff. On the other hand Beth was thinking, *This girl needs to quicken her pace or she will never catch up with me.*

They got the tickets and boarded the train. Anna explained the plan to Beth, "We will go to the library first. When we get there we can look up the orphanage records, the definition of deciduous and see if there is anything about your parents in the news."

The train slowly ran over the tracks, bumping every so often, sending a tremor through the train. The only entertainment was the cows grazing on the endless fields of grass. This was ever so boring for Anna so she pulled out a book and started reading. Beth had other ideas. "Look at this," Beth requested as she pulled the portraits she had drawn out of her backpack. She was hoping that Anna knew something that could help her with this problem of not remembering who the baby was since she seemed like a very smart girl.

"Cool," Anna said vaguely without looking up from her book.

"No, seriously, look," Beth said and explained her predicament to Anna.

"Well, I remember reading about people remembering parts of a memory, but not all of it. It has happened to me before and my theory is the person was so young when it happened that they can only remember part of it, but we could look up more about it at the library," said Anna.

Satisfied, Beth pulled out some more sketching tools and started doodling. Eventually they got to the town. They both charged towards the library. Pedestrians gave them appalled looks, but they didn't care. They were both free. Anna was free from the orphanage and Beth was free from her parents' watchful eye.

In some ways Beth and Anna felt very differently about family. They both thought it was very important, but Beth had always taken family for granted until now. Anna had always wished to have a family and Beth had always wished to be free just for a little while from her overprotective parents.

They trekked to the library. It was very far away from the train station. They walked and walked and walked and walked and walked. As they were walking Beth was contemplating her parents and noticed that her mother's name, Annabeth could be made by putting together Anna and Beth. She mentioned this to Anna.

"Hmph," Anna grumbled, but that might have been because of the cold. It was soon pouring down rain and the girls were soaking wet and freezing.

It was soon afternoon and both girls were chilled to the bone. Eventually, after what seemed like hours, they arrived at the library. They tied Mr. Fluffy Pants in front of the library and put Sheila and their bags by the door. They both walked into the warm, heated environment and sighed.

They must have sighed rather loudly because the librarian at the desk laughed and said "Have you girls been out in that rain all day?" She had a tight bun of dark hair and her eyes sparkled with friendliness.

The girls were grateful for some kindness and both said, "Yes."

"Well then!" the librarian sympathized. "Let's get you two a good book. What did you have in mind?" Beth explained what she was looking for while Anna searched for information they were looking for on the computer.

Beth found that the librarian was rather snappy if you got something wrong or misunderstood. This happened a lot, because the book titled _Recovering Repressed Memories_ had a lot of big words in it. After about thirty minutes Beth decided to call it quits, she told the librarian that they would come back tomorrow to do more research. Beth didn't tell the librarian they probably wouldn't be there tomorrow if Anna found anything important. She felt a little bad lying to an adult, but it had to be done if she and Anna wanted to find their parents.

As Anna and Beth walked out of the library Beth told Anna what she had promised the librarian. Anna seemed mad about that. She muttered to herself, "Never make a promise you know you can't keep." It took Beth a few minutes to realize that Anna was talking about her parents, not just the librarian. She immediately felt bad and wished she had never brought up the subject. She understood that Anna's parents made a promise they couldn't keep and Anna was angry at them for that, but they would have to keep going if they wanted to ever find them.

"So did you find anything important on the computer?" Beth changed the subject quickly. She didn't want to offend Anna any further.

"Well the orphanage records were labeled as 'private' and I couldn't view them. There wasn't much on your parents, just that they had disappeared. The most interesting thing that I found was the definition of deciduous," Anna explained. "It means shedding leaves each year."

Beth looked at her, "And when you say shedding leaves you mean..."

"A forest," Anna finished for her. "My guess is your parents worked as accountants for my parents and something happened to them both which made them leave a message to us. They didn't think that we would find each other, so they left us both clues to help us find them even if we hadn't met each other. The closest deciduous forest is the one right over there." Anna pointed to the forest behind the library.

Without consulting each other, they gathered their belongings and walked into the dark expanse of forest without a clue of what was ahead of them. If they were to find their parents they would need to go into this forest and they would do anything to find their parents.

The forest consisted of lush greenery, beautiful high trees and a river. They slipped and slid down the muddy banks in search for their parents.

"So what are we looking for here?" Anna asked Beth.

"Well, any sign of our parents or any other humans for that matter," she whispered, looking around at their beautiful, but humanless, surroundings. A branch creaked next to Anna and she stumbled. The slippery mud gave way under her and she tumbled right into the rushing river below them. "Anna!" Beth screamed, but the water had already carried her too far down the stream to hear her. The river was rushing around her and she was dunked under the water many times. She remembered from a book she read that she shouldn't stand up because her foot might get caught in a rock and she could get pulled under. She calmly swam to the bank and sat down. Sheila yowled in agitation from inside her cat carrier. Anna guessed that she was soaking wet, her cat carrier wasn't very waterproof.

Now she had lost her new friend on her journey because of nature. Beautiful, calm, breathtaking nature had done this to her. Anna was sure that Beth would find her parents and walk out of the forest, leaving Anna all alone without any family. That was her, Anna, forever the girl with no family, no friends, no anyone.

She looked around. There was no use in looking for Beth now, it would soon be too dark to see anything. She had to find some shelter and food if she wanted to survive. There was no way she would go back to the orphanage and there was nowhere left on the earth where she was welcome. She might as well live here. Just as she was meant to, by herself.

She found a cave and went in to explore it. It was very roomy and she could fit herself and her possessions with space to sleep and be comfortable. The cave had some sub-caves for different rooms and it was as cozy as a cave could be. She decided that the room farthest from the opening would be her bedroom so she wouldn't be very cold at night.

She carefully set up the room. Luckily she had most of her things in a waterproof bag, so her bed covers were dry. She placed them in a corner of the room and she set her books and report cards in another. She decided that she would try and make a shelf for them later on. She soon realized that the cave would be a target for bears and other unfriendly animals and quickly covered up the door with some tree wood that was strong and sturdy. Thinking of all the wonderful things she would add to her new home the next day, she fell asleep.

Four

The next morning Anna woke with a start as
she realized she wasn't in one of the orphanage's
cozy beds, but on the cold stone floor of a cave. It
took her a moment to remember all that had
happened yesterday. She tried to forget how alone
she felt as she started to work. Anna wanted to make
sure that Beth wasn't still in the forest before she
gave up all hope on her new friend, so she started to
walk up river to the find where she left Beth. After
around twenty minutes of climbing over logs and
fallen branches Anna finally reached her destination.
Beth was nowhere to be seen. Anna sighed and
turned around to head back to the cave, maybe Beth
had left her behind.

When Anna arrived at the cave, she decided
that she needed to make it feel more like home. The
walls seemed dark and unforgiving so she decided
that first she would add a little color to them. There
was no way Anna could live in this place without
some decoration, otherwise, she would just be living
in a cave, not a home. So she set to work picking
flowers and fruits off trees. Soon she had a vast
assortment of plant life and greenery for decoration.
She hung them up on the wall and door.

It was noon when she was alerted to her
need for food by her growling stomach. Anna
looked over at the river and realized that the thing

that had taken her away from Beth and her hope of family might also be her savior. Medium sized fish swam lazily in the small pools of water that diverged from the river. They would be the easiest to get to and possibly the only source of meat in the forest that Anna would be able to catch.

Anna took a long, light stick and cut the end into a point with her pocket knife. After she was finished she sat down on a flat, smooth rock and waited for a fish.

She waited for a long time with many unsuccessful attempts. Birds called to each other across the trees, startling Anna every time she came close to catching a fish. Suddenly a streak of silver flashed by and her instincts took over. She stabbed her homemade spear into the water; when she pulled it out, it had a wriggling fish on the end.

Anna was thoroughly satisfied with the progress she had made in just a day and decided to call it a night. She retreated into her cave and started a fire with some matches and wood. Anna cleaned out the fish and set it over the fire to cook.

Anna had been ready for a situation like this, her plan B was to live like this if there was no family out there for her, so she had brought survival books with tips for living in the wild. She smiled to herself. Yep, that was her, always planning ahead.

Sheila slunk into the room and curled up in the moss Anna had set out for her, but not after shooting an annoyed look in Anna's direction. She had been sulking in one of the back caves since their trip down the river.

The cave felt more like a home to Anna now, with the soothing crackling of the flame and the soft shadows cast by the fire. For the first time in a while she thought of Beth. Beth had probably fled back to the town to her aunt. Anna felt hollow inside at that thought. She had believed that Beth was going to be a good friend, one that would help her find her parents.

Thinking of friends made Anna remember the orphanage. Although they didn't have much, Anna always knew that Ms. Melvins did her best for the girls. With a pang, she remembered Charlene.

Charlene had always been there for her and other girls who felt left out. She always had her straight blond hair tied back in a ponytail and Anna could almost see her now. Charlene could easily have been in the popular group at school. She had been invited many times, but had always turned down the offer. She had always preferred helping others and gaining friends through trust rather than her height on the totem pole. Charlene had been best friends with Anna since she came to the orphanage eleven years ago and Anna wondered if they would ever meet again. Anna sighed, she knew that she couldn't dwell on the past. She needed to keep moving forward, otherwise she would be living in the past forever.

Now she had a perfect life here with the necessities of survival and comfortable living. Food, books, shelter, a bed (kind of), pocket knife and Sheila. By the time all this thinking was done, the fish had cooked and Anna could eat. After she had eaten the fish she put out the fire with water from the river and blocked the entrance. As she pulled the covers over her, she glowed with pride at how much she had accomplished in just one day.

Five

The next morning Anna woke to the harsh whistling of cold wind. She sat up in terror. She shouldn't be hearing wind, the door to the cave was closed. Sheila! Sheila could have easily escaped if the door was open. She raced through the cave looking for Sheila, but she was nowhere to be seen. Horror coursed through her. How could she have let Sheila escape? Had some wild animal broken in and taken her? Anna rushed outside, not bothered by the wind rushing around her and freezing her.

"Sheila!" she called frantically "Sheila!" Sheila was nowhere in sight and Anna was on the verge of giving up. She plopped down on the rock she had fished on yesterday and started to cry. How could she have let her lifelong friend, her only family just disappear? Anna shielded herself from the rain and wind and curled up on the rock. Her tears froze as they slid down her cheeks.

Suddenly she heard a creak in the woods like an animal stepping on a stick. Could it be Sheila or Beth? Might it be the animal that took Sheila coming back? Anna looked up just in time to see Sheila prance out of the forest with three enormous fish in her jaws. Anna cried out in happiness and ran over to her pet. After a few minutes of greeting, Sheila decided it was too cold for her and bounded inside.

Anna practically skipped inside and carefully patched up the hole Sheila had escaped out of. She cleaned and cooked the fish, putting two away in storage. After Anna blocked the storage in response to the sly and hungry look on Sheila's face, they shared one fish for breakfast and warmed themselves up by the fire. It had been a big morning and Anna was frozen, not just by the storm raging outside, but the day's terrifying events.

After several days in her new home Anna encountered a problem. It was often so stormy and windy outside she couldn't collect fresh water from the river. Sheila and Anna could go for a couple of days without water, but it wasn't the most pleasant experience. So one sunny day Anna decided that she would redirect the route of the river into the cave so she could collect water anytime she wanted even if it was too cold and windy to go outside.

This job was going to take a while even if the stone of the cave floor was softer than most. Anna sat down on the floor of the cave and started to scrape a rock against the floor. Hopefully, it would create a shallow enough stream for water to flow through into one of the smaller caves.

As she scraped the rock over and over again on the floor of the cave, she thought a little bit more of the orphanage. Although the cave was now her home, she missed the orphanage. It had been her home for eleven years and now it felt like a missing piece in her heart.

It was a small building, with two stories. The walls were painted a warm brown that had started peeling years before Anna was born. Although its appearance was not altogether pleasant, it had been a home for the sixteen girls that lived there. Eight girls shared one of the bedrooms and eight girls shared the other. They had four bunk beds in each of the rooms, one up against each wall with room in the middle for playing games and doing schoolwork. On the bottom floor was a bathroom, kitchen, dining room and Ms. Melvins bedroom/office.

It had not been an easy decision to leave her home, but Anna didn't regret it. She knew this was her place. Still, after hours of banging a rock against the floor, she went to bed with not only aching arms, but an aching heart.

The next morning when she woke up her hands and arms still burned from yesterday. She had made progress on the redirection of the water so, after a few hours, she decided to take a break. Water was already trickling into the pool at the end. Soon there would be enough water for her and Sheila to drink, so they wouldn't have to go days without water.

This thought cheered Anna up and she started working again. Soon the water was flowing faster and the cave was filling up. Anna was proud of her work, now her new forest life would be more comfortable.

Six

Anna woke from her sleep excited. This was it! It was her birthday! Normally Anna wouldn't feel especially happy about her birthday because the orphanage didn't have enough money to celebrate sixteen birthdays a year, but today was different. Today she was going to throw herself the best party she could. She might even give herself a present. Anna raced outside. She felt like she could run around the world and be back in time to see Sheila finish her morning snack.

She grabbed Sheila, who only protested for a second, and walked into the forest. Anna decided that she would have some berries for dinner along with some fish.

Suddenly she heard a noise like a stick breaking under the weight of an animal or human. Anna paused and saw a glimpse of caramel brown hair. Someone might be trying to find her. Anna had run from park rangers on more than one occasion, worried they would take her back to the orphanage.

The world whizzed past her as she fled full speed back to the cave, *her* cave. She couldn't let them take this sanctuary from her. As the last branch fell into place over her door, she relaxed. Anna was absolutely sure her cave was camouflaged enough so that even the sharpest eye would pass right over it.

Once even *she* had lost the entrance to the cave! That was a near disaster.

Anna waited in the cave for hours in case the person came back. It was dark out when she finally decided it was safe, too dark in to go searching for any more berries. Anna sighed and looked at the calendar she had carved into the wall. That was the only reason she had known it was her birthday. Now she would have to wait another year for her birthday to come again. *Hopefully that one will go better,* Anna thought as she climbed into bed.

Anna got over her ruined birthday quickly and she even got a present from Sheila the next day.

Anna heard a scratching at the door and chuckled. She stopped laughing when she saw the little "present" Sheila had brought her. It was a bird; a terrified blue jay. Anna gasped and scooped up the bird. It was the cutest thing she had ever seen in her life (not including Sheila, of course). She laid it down on Sheila's bed of moss. It looked unhurt, just paralyzed by fear. Anna sighed in relief and started gathering some supplies. If this bird was going to have a home when she woke Anna would have to work fast.

Anna smiled to herself as she finished her work. *And not a moment too soon,* she thought as she saw the bird shudder. Gently Anna placed the blue jay into her new home. It was wonderful considering that Anna didn't have much time. It was a large cage at least as big as Anna, made of some sturdy branches and leaves. It had three stories for the bird to hop around in. The bottom had food and water, the middle had some toys and the top had a little nest. The bird hopped around the cage and finally settled down in the nest and went to sleep.

Anna whispered to the bird, "I think I'll call you June." She hung the bird cage to the roof of the cave. Then she noticed Sheila slink in. "Oh no you don't!" Anna exclaimed as she shooed her out. "Thanks for the birthday present," she said more playfully. Anna smiled when Sheila gave her moss bed a suspicious sniff that night.

It was only a few days after Sheila had brought June to Anna that she brought her an even smaller baby bird. *The little bird looks only three months old,* Anna speculated, *maybe less. I guess she fell out of her nest.* Since there was no way Anna could get the bird back to her nest, she decided to keep her. As she gently placed the little bird in the cage June woke up. "There's your new friend June. Be good to her. Her name is Belle."

Anna jumped out of bed enthusiastically and went to check her calendar. She had lived exactly one year in the cave and was never found once. So many things had happened in just one year. She had accidentally lost the entrance to the cave because it was so well camouflaged. Sheila brought her June and Belle. Sheila escaped on only the second day.

Seven

Anna heard a crack. She stepped back from her view of the town and looked down. She had come here many times and imagined what it would be like to have a family and do normal things like shopping or going to the movies.

Underneath the tree Anna was perched in was a family of a brother, a sister, a father and a mother. They were laughing and playing. That was something that Anna had never been able to do with her family. She watched them walk down the sidewalk and step into a big house at the end of the street.

As Anna walked back to the cave she thought about what it would be like to have her family back. They would laugh, play and celebrate holidays together. They would be a family.

It was not long after her one year anniversary of getting washed down the river that Anna started getting more and more comfortable with venturing out of the cave and into the forest. One day she was out with Sheila and she heard a crack up in the trees. When Anna looked up she saw nothing, but decided to investigate. She had heard too many sounds in this area for it just to be a coincidence.

Anna told Sheila to stay although she knew it would never work and started climbing up the tree.

She had practiced climbing trees many times so she would have an easy escape if she were caught by a park ranger or an animal, but still every branch she went up she was more fearful that she would plummet to the ground. She was so careful that she didn't notice the structure above her until her head banged against it.

Anna was so surprised that she slipped off the branch and fell. The branches flew past her and scraped her arms and legs. Terror rushed through her and suddenly it all stopped. Something grabbed her arm and pulled her up onto the branch. Once she had regained her senses she looked for her savior. She was greeted with two very familiar sparkling blue eyes.

Eight

"Beth?!" Anna gasped.

"You're welcome." Beth giggled "It's a good thing I was there to catch you. Now follow me." She climbed up the tree like a monkey and Anna clumsily followed her. When they reached the wood Anna had banged her head against, Beth led Anna through a gap. When Anna had finished struggling in Beth said "Ta da!" Anna was stunned; before her was a tree house.

"You made this?" Anna asked. How could Beth have made this by herself?

"No, I found it here." She showed Anna around the tree house; it had a dining room and bedroom. "Well, actually I made the little elevator for Mr. Fluffy Pants."

"But I thought you left." Anna exclaimed.

"Leave? When I still had a friend in the forest and possibly parents too?" Beth asked. Anna immediately felt guilty for all the things she had thought that Beth would do once they were separated.

"Come on, I want to show you something." Anna said. They bounded through the forest and Beth surprised Anna again.

"I've seen you before this." Anna was so breathless she could only give Beth a questioning look. "Remember when you were in the forest picking berries? I think I surprised you and you ran away before you saw me. I tried to follow you, but I didn't see anything by the river to give away you were there."

Anna was both surprised and proud, "I was picking berries for dinner. I camouflaged the entrance to my home so no one would see it."

"Why wouldn't you want anyone to see it?"

"Well, what if a park ranger came and made us go home? It isn't exactly legal for a girl to run away and live in a forest."

"Good point." They ran for a little while more until they came to Anna's home. "So where is it?" Beth asked.

"Look," Anna answered. They stood there for several minutes as Beth inspected the forest around them.

Finally she gave up, "I can't see anything." Anna removed the cover of the entrance and enthusiastically led Beth around her cave showing her all of the rooms. Beth felt a little let down. She felt as if the cave walls were crushing her and even though Anna had decorated some of the cave walls, there was still too much blank space for Beth. She still told Anna she loved it because she didn't want to hurt her feelings.

They talked for a bit more before Beth mentioned, "I think this will be pretty fun. Two girls living together in a forest, it sounds like something out of a book. Still, I'm not sure that it beats living in my aunt's orphanage with sixteen other girls."

"What did you say?" Anna looked at her. She needed to make sure that she had heard Beth correctly, knowing that there could only be so many orphanages with sixteen girls in it in their area.

"My aunt runs an orphanage with sixteen orphaned..." Beth trailed off when she saw the look on Anna's face.

"What is your aunt's name?" Anna asked quietly.

"Ruth Melvins." Beth studied Anna questioningly. "What's wrong?"

"Ms. Melvins, she ran the orphanage I lived in before I left."

Once Anna got over her shock, she decided that there could be a simple answer to the coincidence. "I think that Ms. Melvins gave me the note at the request of your parents, believing that they would meet up and become friends and soon figure out the code. The note was never from my parents," she realized. Anna couldn't believe that this had been taken away from as well. Her parents hadn't given her the note, she was just being used by Beth's parents and aunt.

After she explained this theory to Beth, she replied, "That would make sense, but I would still like to stay in the forest in case my parents show up."

"Of course!" Anna exclaimed like there was no other option. Even though her heart was aching because of the sudden realization that her parents weren't in the forest and were probably never going to find her.

"My parents can help," Beth said gently.

"I know." Anna shook her head and put on an unconvincing smile. "I think you should head back, it is getting dark."

"Yeah," Beth agreed reluctantly and got up. She walked towards the door, but turned around before she got there. "Everything will be okay," she tried to reassure Anna.

Anna looked up at her and gave her a sad look. "Everything will be okay for you," she corrected. "I don't know about me." She got up and retreated to her bedroom before Beth could respond.

The next day, Anna woke to knocking on her door. At first she was worried it was the police or park rangers, but when she cautiously opened the door, Beth stood there. She had as many layers on as you could possibly imagine on and she was holding a coat. "Here put it on." Beth thrust the coat at Anna. "You'll need it." Anna looked behind Beth and saw that it was snowing.

The snow was piled at least a foot high and everywhere Sheila and Mr. Fluffy Pants stepped they sank into the snow until you could only see their little heads poking out. The girls laughed themselves silly as the animals shot them disgruntled looks. It was a nice change for Anna, who had spent most of the night before sitting in silence, thinking about her parents.

They played until they couldn't feel their hands. When they finally decided to go inside Anna brought in a bucket of water and warmed it up. While it was boiling she crushed some berries and put the powder in the water. Once it was finished both girls had a cup of tea in their hands.

It kept snowing for many days after that and one of those days Anna had a brilliant idea. "An igloo?" Beth asked.

"Yes, an igloo," Anna replied. "It would be fun and we could build it in between the cave and the tree house so we wouldn't have to walk so far meet each other. Also…"

"Okay, okay you convinced me. Let's do it," Beth interrupted. "I have a box in the tree house that we could use to make the blocks for the igloo."

"Okay," Anna said, "I'll go get it." She walked along the trail to Beth's house and picked up the box from the corner of the tree house.

When Anna got back she discovered Beth making a little igloo for their pets. "What?" she asked when Anna gave her a look.

When they finished it was more of a square shaped igloo, but neither of the girls really cared. "What if we built tunnels out of snow leading to the tree house, the igloo and the cave? It wouldn't take a lot more time than the igloo even if they are far apart," Beth proposed. Anna agreed and they started to work.

By then it was about noon and the girls were tired. The cold snow felt refreshing on their hands as they worked on the tunnels. They were about halfway done when they had to go home because it was sunset. It was agreed that they would continue in the morning.

The next morning the girls met at the ending point from the day before. It was hard work, but the girls were determined. Making an igloo was more fun than sitting in the cave or the tree house. At about noon they were done. The girls stepped back to admire their work. Beth felt her foot slide out from under her on the ice. She slipped and slid until she fell into the freezing cold river. It was only a second before her entire body went numb.

Nearby on the shore Anna remembered when she was washed down the river. She couldn't let that happen to Beth. They might never see each other again! She had to do something. Just as Anna started to formulate a plan, Beth grabbed a rock and pulled herself to safety. She was shivering all over and she shattered "I… I request a b…blanket."

Anna giggled to herself and went inside to get a blanket for Beth. Once Beth was warmed up, the girls parted ways through the snow tunnel.

Nine

It had been two years since Anna left the orphanage and she was now fifteen. Anna was very excited for the big celebration Beth had planned for her birthday. However, it seemed as if Beth had forgotten the party. Actually, it seemed as if she had forgotten to get out of bed as well.

Anna decided to find Beth. She walked along the well-worn path leading to Beth's tree house and remembered the time when part of their snow fort collapsed, leaving Anna cut off from her home. It had taken them about half an hour to dig themselves out.

When she reached the tree house and called up there was no answer. Suddenly she was scared. What if something had happened to Beth? She climbed up the tree as swiftly as she could and searched the house. There was no sign of Beth anywhere.

Anna sat down on one of the kitchen chairs in despair. Where was she? *Mr. Fluffy Pants isn't here so it must mean that he is with Beth,* Anna thought, *Everything looks normal. The chairs are set around the table neatly, the books are color coordinated on the bookshelf, all her drawings are placed with clear tape around the wall and there is that random piece of paper sitting on the counter over there and the…* Anna backtracked quickly.

Beth always left her tree house in perfect order so the note was probably a clue! Anna opened the note and read,

We were once stuck here and your next clue is too.

A scavenger hunt! It must mean the place where the girls were caved in that time in winter. Anna ran towards the place where the tunnels were before they melted. When she got there she found another note sitting under a rock.

The place where our forest adventure started? That's where your next clue is too.

The place where our forest adventure began? That would be the place that Anna was washed down the river. That was very far away. It would take about twenty minutes to get there and twenty minutes to get back. Anna started the trek towards the next clue. *I hope this worth the hike,* Anna thought. After about twenty minutes of huffing and puffing, Anna found the next clue.

I know you were expecting something after walking all the way here, but you will have to come back home, there is a surprise waiting for you there.

Anna laughed inwardly. This was definitely a scavenger hunt to get Anna away from the cave so Beth could plan something. It was a funny joke, but now Anna would have to hike all the way back. She sighed and turned around.

Ten

Anna was panting when she finally got home. It had taken much longer than she had expected to get back. Beth was sitting outside the cave humming to herself. She looked up when she noticed Anna and said, "So how was the scavenger hunt?"

"It would have been a tiny bit better if you had warned me before hand it was going to take an hour," Anna grumbled.

Beth laughed cheerfully and led her inside. "Come on I want to show you something."

Anna gasped when she saw what was inside. Beth had painted a mural on her wall. It was beautiful. Anna couldn't even explain it in words because it was all so abstract.

"Thank you! It's so pretty," Anna told Beth. "I suggest asking your parents before giving it to them as an anniversary present." Beth giggled.

"What did you paint it with?" Anna asked.

"My secret family recipe," Beth said proudly.

"Really?" Anna asked.

"No, of course not," Beth scoffed. "I mashed up some berries and roots. By the way, what day is it? I can't really keep a calendar. I only knew it was your birthday because you told me."

When Anna told her she gasped. "We have the same birthday!" Beth said excitedly. "That's a big coincidence."

"Don't you think we've seen too many coincidences?" Anna picked up a rock and started writing on the wall facing the mural.

1. Anna and Beth together makes Annabeth (Beth's mother's name)

2. Same birthday

3. Ms. Melvins (head of orphanage) is one of Beth's aunts

4. Note from both of our parents

Suddenly Anna had an idea, "Beth show me those drawings again." Beth obliged, showing Anna the baby pictures she had been drawing. Anna pulled the photos of herself as a two year old at the orphanage out of her pocket. She held them up next to each other.

"So similar," Beth whispered.

"Exactly!" Anna said excitedly. "My baby picture and your drawing look so similar we must have known each other as babies. Maybe we were born in the same hospital on the same day and you saw me." She added to the list,

5. Anna's baby picture and Beth's drawing

"Bravo, bravo," said a mysterious voice from the shadows. Both girls were startled by the unexpected voice. The woman stepped out of the shadows and said, "But I'm afraid that I will still have to arrest you."

Eleven

It is not every day that a strange woman walks into your home and tells you that she will arrest you. Both girls were speechless. The woman looked amused at their faces and explained, "I'm July Melvins." This broke the silence.

"July Melvins! Are you related to Beth's mom? That was her maiden name," Anna exclaimed as she looked toward Beth.

"Yes, I am your mother's sister, but that is all I will say here," July Melvins said, looking around in disgust at the cave. "If you want to hear any more you will have to come with me."

Anna looked at Beth and both girls knew they would have to work together if they wanted to get out of this. Beth asked slowly, "Why are we being arrested? We didn't do anything wrong did we?"

"Oh we just need to get something figured out." The voices faded as Anna inched into her bedroom. She quickly packed up everything she could and made sure that Sheila was following her. As she inched back into the room she saw that July Melvins and Beth were face to face, obviously arguing about something.

"Beth!" Anna yelled. "Let's go!" They both slipped out of the cave and ran as far as they could. They ran all the way to the tree house and climbed up. They only relaxed once they were in the tree house.

"Do you think she knows about the tree house too?" Beth asked breathlessly. Anna was close to tears. *What are they going to do with June and Belle?* Beth didn't seem to notice. She was bustling around the kitchen making a cup of tea. "Well, I guess that we will just have to wait and find out. If we escaped once we will be able to again," Beth answered her own question. "What do you think she meant when she said she was going to arrest us?" Once again, Anna didn't answer. "Gosh it's like talking to myself here," Beth said loudly.

Anna didn't even look up, all her hard work was gone. She had been working on the cave for one year and now it was all gone. The birds, pond, and furniture were all gone. She had worked so hard to make that cave her home and now she had lost it. She wondered if she would ever have a home. Anna felt numb with loss. At least she had Sheila with her. If she had lost her too, Anna wouldn't know what to do.

"There you go." Beth set down some tea on the table in front of Anna. Anna just seemed lost in thought. Beth was exasperated at Anna's behavior and tried again, "What do you think we should do now? Anna?"

"Hmm? Oh yes that. Well I think that most people in this situation would avoid being arrested."

This was not the answer Beth was looking for, and she knew what Anna was planning. "She knows about the cave Anna, I don't think you should go back there."

"I want to see if she is still there." Anna climbed down the tree and walked along the path to her cave before Beth could stop her. She wanted to see if July Melvins was still there and if she could sneak in to see her birds. Anna could see no sign of anyone near the cave so she entered.

It was obvious that everything had been searched. She had only been able to grab a few things before their escape. Just clothes, bed covers and pocket knife. All the books in her room had been searched and her report cards had been ripped open. Obviously nothing had been of too much interest because it was all still there.

She checked the bird cave. There in the cave was just one bird, Belle. What had they done with June? Anna knew there was no way she could carry the cage with Belle in it all the way to the tree house. She slowly approached the cage and opened it. Belle hopped around for a moment and looked at Anna as if to say, *Are you sure about this?* After a few seconds Belle hopped out and took flight. She was out of the cave before Anna had time to even say goodbye.

"Perfect, perfect. I knew you would come back," July Melvins appeared from the shadows.

Anna was mad. "Okay, first of all what did you do with June and second what is it with you and sneaking up on people?"

"Who is June? Oh, June is the bird. You will find out where she is if you come with me."

But Anna was already too far away to hear her. The birds chirped in the bright and lush trees as Anna ran to the tree house. She had to warn Beth. Just before she reached she saw two familiar birds sitting on a branch. It was Belle and June! They had both escaped and found each other. Anna waved at them. Both of the birds chirped at her and flew off. Anna turned around and hurried on. Bright colors and noises burst from every tree just as it usually did. Suddenly it all stopped and Anna knew something was about to happen, but this just made her run faster.

"Beth!" Anna yelled up the tree. "We have to hurry. She saw me in the cave."

Beth's head appeared in the hole in the floor of the tree house. "Anna why didn't you listen to me?"

Anna had no words to answer this and she just yelled, "We have to go!" It had been only a few months ago when Anna and Beth were reunited and now they would have to continue their journey somewhere else. *It's all my fault*, Anna thought.

Beth was thinking while she packed her stuff, *I should have stopped her*. Beth nimbly climbed down the tree like she had done it thousands of times before and she probably had.

"Beth, I'm," Anna stopped when a bright light flashed in the sky, blinding both girls. By the time they could see again they were in a dark, metal chain net. "sorry!" Anna tried to finish her sentence over the roar of helicopter blades.

Twelve

July Melvins led the girls down a dark hallway. Suddenly the lights flickered on and the girls could see the white hallway leading down to a door. Beth hated white space and she had so many ideas to brighten this place up she could barely stop herself from exploding with them.

Once they were at the door, July Melvins entered the room beckoning for Anna and Beth to follow her. She sat down. "So you have found all the clues your parents left for you." This seemed directed at both girls so they didn't know who she was talking about. Before they could ask, July Melvins continued, "Let me show you the list." On a white board she wrote,

1. Anna and Beth make the name Annabeth (mother)

2. Baby picture and Beth's drawing are similar

3. Ms. Melvins

4. Note from parents

5. Same birthday

"You've seen the connection, but I can't believe you haven't figured it out yet," July Melvins finished. "Here I'll tell you the whole story." She said it like she was being generous. It disgusted Beth.

"You two are fraternal twins and I'll prove it. Once upon a time my sister, who is also your mother, threatened to tell the government about what I do down here because it is illegal. I took Anna and placed her in an orphanage with my other sister, Ruth. I said I would keep you safe for as long as I could and be a proper aunt if they just did one thing for me."

"Never tell anyone," Anna finished her sentence bitterly, "but the notes didn't match in handwriting, how could they both be written by Beth's mom?" She still didn't want to believe this woman.

Their aunt smiled sweetly. "Your mother could have easily changed her handwriting for your note."

"What about our names?" Anna asked.

"Before I separated you, sweet Annabeth named you two hoping that someday if you found each other somehow you would know the truth. Haven't you two noticed that you had the same last name? Recently, I found that your parents were trying to figure out a loophole in our agreement. They were very close to finding it so I placed them on a remote island where nobody will ever find them. They are perfectly safe. Your parents found out I was planning on capturing them and they left Beth the note hoping you would know where to go. She asked my other sister to give the note to Anna, because they hoped that you two would become friends at the orphanage. I had always hoped that Ruth wouldn't help them, but I guess that helping me was never an option for her."

"I remember," Beth gasped. "It was the night after our second birthday and our parents..."

"...had just put us to bed," Anna said, almost as if she was in a trance. "I was about to fall asleep, then there was a crash. I..."

"...looked over at the window and saw a woman," Beth whispered. "She looked like mother, just a little bit and..."

"...I laughed. It seemed preposterous to me that anybody but me and my..."

"...sister could look alike at all. The woman looked around the room until her eyes..."

"...came to us. When she saw us she grinned. It was an..."

"...evil grin, almost an insane grin. She walked over to..."

"...my crib and picked me up, I was..."

"...scared. What was she doing with my sister? I wailed and..."

"...the woman looked over to the door. She was scared she would be caught, so she..."

"...bounded to the window. I screamed louder and our parents..."

"...rushed into the room, but it was too late, I was already gone."

"How interesting," July exclaimed like they were an experiment. "I believe we have a case of repressed memory here. So neither of you could remember anything about that night?"

"Just the drawings," Beth shook her head. She was still shocked at everything that they had missed. How was it possible that they hadn't noticed they had the same last names?

"And the dreams," Anna said. "The sound of glass crashing against the floor, the wailing baby, the shadow over my bed..."

Beth looked over at her new-found sister in concern and saw a tear slide down her cheek.

"What are you going to do with us now?" Beth asked, furious at her aunt for... everything.

"Why I'm so glad you asked. I will take you to the remote island so you can live the rest of your life happily and never tell anyone of what I'm doing here."

"We don't even know what you are doing here," Beth protested.

"However you do know that something is happening here and that is enough reason to put you on the island. We couldn't have you telling the police. I'll just put you on the cruise ship to Hawaii with one of my employees, where you will go missing. Then she will fly you to the island."

"What are the coordinates? I keep track of the weather near here and if there is really windy weather I will get airsick," Beth lied easily. After July told her she pretended to think about it and said, "I think that will be okay." Beth had a feeling that she was going to need those coordinates.

July Melvins led them out of the room and into the hallway where her employee was waiting to take them. As she led the girls out of the facility both girls were thinking hard. Once the woman turned her back both girls bolted for the forest. Dark trees and muddy branches flew past the girls as they galloped through the forest. When they reached the tree house and climbed to safety, there was a surprise waiting for them. The tree house had been searched up and down and everything that made the tree house suitable for living was taken out. All they had now was Sheila, Mr. Fluffy Pants and the two bags of supplies they had been carrying.

"We could go check the cave," Beth suggested half-heartedly, but Anna knew it wasn't a good idea. July Melvins had probably already done the same thing there or set a trap there just as she had before.

"We can't," Anna said.

Beth now understood why Anna had acted that way earlier. Her home was taken away now too. She sat down on the floor in despair. "So now you know how it feels to have your home taken away! Of course you couldn't have been more considerate when it happened to me, could you?" Anna shouted at Beth and stormed out of the tree house.

Beth hardly even looked up at the sound. Anna rushed out into the rain which was now pouring down making the dirt muddy and the leaves slick. After running for a couple of minutes, Anna reached the edge of the forest. She slipped behind the trees and sat down on a rock. Anna ducked out of sight when she saw a family heading her way on the sidewalk. She realized it was the same family she had seen walking by the forest not long before she found Beth.

"Mama!" the little boy shrieked. "I saw something move." He pointed straight at Anna's rock.

"Oh it was nothing," the mother comforted the little boy.

Meanwhile the older sister shouted, "I bet it was a bear. Can we go catch it and sell it to the zoo?"

She was so adorable and serious at the same time Anna guessed she was about seven or eight years old. The father picked up the little girl and swung her around. The family was so happy it made Anna's heart break. She hadn't had a real family for eleven years and just when she had found her sister she had probably already lost her. She took a deep breath and left the family to decide whether or not they should sell the bear to the zoo.

All the way back Anna tried out different versions of her apology to Beth in her head. When Anna finally got to the tree house and found Beth sitting in the same place she was when Anna left, all Anna said was, "I think we have something to do. You wrote down those coordinates, right?"

Thirteen

The next day Anna and Beth were ready to go. They only had their pets and enough money to get them to the coordinates July had given them. Both girls still felt a little awkward about what happened the night before, but neither had said anything yet. Finally Anna said, "I'm sorry about last night. I didn't mean that."

"No, that's fine. I should have been nice when it happened to you," Beth answered stiffly. She was obviously not happy about it yet. Anna sighed. She didn't know how else to apologize to Beth. She was going to have to understand eventually that Anna was sorry.

They walked to the library for the first time in two years. "A bit late, aren't you?" the librarian asked with a smile on her face.

The girls grinned nervously. "Um, we got a bit side tracked," Beth tried to explain.

"For two years?" The librarian smiled as if she understood everything.

"We would like to look at a map," Anna asked. "Please." They looked at the maps for a while and found the coordinates on a map. There wasn't anything that could signify an island at the location.

"We have to try," Anna said. "We can rent a boat to get there, it's not too far away." Beth agreed. They thanked the librarian and walked out.

The dock was only a few minutes away. While they walked, they were silent. Beth had obviously not gotten over Anna's outburst the other day. "Look, I really am sorry about what happened last night," Anna said.

Beth looked at her and sighed, "I know." Anna felt satisfied now and it seemed like Beth was too.

When they got to the dock, they rented a boat. The water splashed up against the deck and white foam was rocking the boat back and forth. Anna navigated with a GPS that came with the boat and Beth paddled.

As they traveled further and further into the dark sea, the tension grew in the boat. It was most likely because of the warning the man who rented the boat gave to them. He had told them that nobody ever came back from the place they were attempting to find. Neither girl had talked for hours except to navigate or switch jobs.

Soon Beth was green and seasick. Her family hardly ever traveled by boat. They could afford luxury airlines and private jets.

Several times they thought they saw a fin slicing through the water, but it turned out to be trash. It seemed like hours before they finally reached land.

Fourteen

The boat bumped over rocks onto shore. They walked around for a little bit and inspected the island. There was nothing to show any sign that their parents were there or that anyone was ever there at all. They scouted around the island for a while, which wasn't very hard. The island was probably about as big as a normal cul-de-sac neighborhood.

"There must be some sort of trapdoor or underwater palace or something," Beth protested.

"Like that cave over there," Anna pointed out a cave in a hillside.

"What is it with you and caves?" Beth grumbled, but she followed Anna anyway.

The cave was like the cave Anna had lived in before she had made it her home. It had dark, lonely walls and many caverns and tunnels connected to the large entrance. They searched them using a trail of leaves so they wouldn't get lost. "It's like the Labyrinth from the old Greek stories," Anna pointed out excitedly. She was always excited to talk about reading and books.

Beth looked lost at this comment and Anna muttered, "Never mind."

The last cave they came upon was circular. It seemed too circular to be made by erosion. A lever stood in the middle. Both girls took turns pulling as hard as they could, but it wouldn't budge. They had to pull together for it to move even an inch. When they finally got it nothing happened.

"That's it?" Anna panted. "Big, huge, obviously man-made lever in the middle of a dark cave on an island untouched by humans and it does nothing?"

"We could check the other rooms and see if it moved a trap door or something. It might have been a fake, there could be a real entrance somewhere else on the island," Beth suggested breathlessly.

"Sure, whatever, do what you want. I'll just sit over here and pretend that I wasn't so close to finding my family for the first time in eleven years and then failed," Anna said dejectedly and flopped down on the cave floor. Beth was hurt. She was Anna's family too.

Ever since they had found out they were sisters, Anna was more distant than when they were friends. Beth wished they had never found their aunt so they would still be living the way they had been before, never knowing they were family, but happy all the same. Knowing they are sisters shouldn't make them drift apart. In fact it should make them closer! Beth inspected some of the caves and thought about this. She was thinking so hard that even if she did find a trap door she would probably have fallen in. Finally after ten minutes she decided she would confront Anna and talk to her. She walked into the cave where she had left Anna.

Beth tried not to look at Anna as she said, "Anna, we are family and family should always stick together." Anna was silent for so long Beth's neck started to get stiff from trying to avoid Anna's gaze. Finally she had to look up. Anna was holding the note their mother had left her. Beth had been so carefree and happy when they had found each other and figured out the code. They had both been. Now she knew it wasn't always like that in the real world.

"Yes family should always stick together, but that doesn't mean they do," Anna finally answered. "Come on. I guess that we have to live here now, just like before."

"What about the boat? We only rented it," Beth asked, trying to find a reason not to stay. She wasn't sure she liked this island or the reason they were staying there.

"No, I bought it instead. I thought we might need it again," Anna explained. Beth sighed, Anna was always thinking ahead. Sometimes it was a blessing and sometimes it was a curse. Anna walked out of the cave and called back to Beth, "Come on, we need to find you a home before dark."

"Why can't I live with you?" Beth whispered. "Family sticks together."

Fifteen

They made a cozy lean-to for Beth. The wood was tightly woven together and kept the air warm so it should have kept Beth warm, but that night she went to sleep with a cold feeling.

It was hard to tell if their stay at the island was like their stay at the forest. Anna would say that they lived exactly the same as before. They caught fish from a river that split the island in two and they gathered plants to make their homes nicer. On the other hand, Beth would say they hardly did any of the things they used to. Anna stayed in her cave most of the day, mostly sulking. Beth tried to walk by Anna's cave every time she walked Mr. Fluffy Pants, but Anna was never in the mood to talk. Bit by bit, Beth began to believe that she no longer had any family in the world. If Anna had known Beth thought this, she would probably say, "I survived thirteen years thinking I had no family. She can survive a few days."

Those few days turned into weeks and months and soon years. When the girls turned sixteen there was no celebration. So much had changed in just a year. The girls had grown more and more distant. Soon they weren't even talking to each other. That's why it took several days for Anna to notice that Beth had disappeared.

She first noticed when she stopped hearing Beth walk her dog past Anna's cave. She ran to the lean-to to check on Beth and found nothing there. It seemed as if Beth had left or someone had taken her somewhere. Anna searched the whole island frantically for Beth, but she could find nothing.

Then she noticed the boat was gone. Anna decided that Beth had left the island on purpose to strand Anna there. All Anna could do now was wait to see if Beth came back or somebody came to rescue her.

When Anna found Mr. Fluffy Pants she was relieved. She knew if Beth was as attached to her dog as she was to Sheila that she would be coming back. That meant Anna would have a chance to tell Beth how sorry she was.

Sixteen

Beth's boat capsized during her journey. She was stranded on the mainland. Beth knew that she probably shouldn't have left the island without telling Anna, but she needed to get away from the island. Sometimes it felt like she was suffocating from the lack of space on the island.

She needed to get enough money to buy a new boat and have somewhere to stay, so she found a job at a solo singing program. She sang at a church. Sometimes the songs she sung at the church reminded her of her parents and how much she missed them. Beth remembered the time when she and her parents would go to fancy restaurants every Saturday and then go out to a movie. This was the routine every Saturday even if there was a meeting her parents needed to go to. They would always make sure Saturday night was for the three of them. Most of the rest of the week they were always home after Beth was asleep and were already gone when she woke up in the morning, but Beth always knew that one of her parents' friends was following her and that she was always being watched. Now she knew why. Her parents were trying to protect her from her aunt.

Every time Beth had been out with her friends and she turned around, someone would be watching her. She had always wished her family would leave her alone, just for a day and now she had gotten her wish. Anna had obviously given up trying to be her friend or her family. She probably didn't even care if Beth was gone two days or five, she might not even notice.

Beth was paid well at her job and soon she had enough money to sail back to the island, but she wasn't sure she wanted to leave. The town was beautiful and she had many friends now. Beth liked the way the town worked together and she found that she loved singing. Many of the people she met thought she was very good at singing, but she knew she couldn't leave Anna stranded on the island. She had already been gone a month.

Beth knew Anna would be furious at her for being gone so long. With a heavy heart Beth sang for the last time at the church, said goodbye to her friends and set off in the boat. The ride back was painstakingly short and Beth wished that she had had more time to compose herself.

When she walked into the cave and saw Anna sitting there, Beth closed her eyes and awaited her wrath. Nothing happened for a few minutes and Beth wondered if Anna had even seen her. She was about to open her eyes when she heard Anna speak. "Do you know how worried I've been?" she asked furiously. "I've waited a month for you! I thought you weren't coming back! Just like them." Anna's anger quickly melted into tears. Beth opened her eyes and found Anna sitting on a rock, sobbing.

Beth sat down next to her and hugged her. Anna tensed for a moment, but relaxed.

They sat there like that for a few minutes, until Anna got up and asked, "So why were you gone so long?" Beth explained her journey. At the end of the story she said, "Well that was a very long shopping spree."

Beth laughed. "Yes, yes it was."

Seventeen

Beth did get her wish. They sailed back to the mainland every once in a while to go on what Anna called shopping sprees. Beth would sing at the church and Anna was a helper at the library. They both enjoyed their jobs and were good friends with people in the town. They would come for the last week of every month. It was like their vacation from living on the island.

Some people would think living on an island without their parents to constantly watch them would be fun, but the fact that their parents weren't watching them was what made them need that little vacation each month.

At the library there was a little girl who Anna thought was so adorable. She came with her parents every Friday. Anna would check out a book for her. The little girl's name was Sara and she loved books. Sara was at a very high reading level for her age. Most of the books she read were at least two hundred and fifty pages long and usually it only took her one month to read them. She and Anna liked to talk about books. They had a little book club on the last Friday of every month.

One time Anna brought Beth along. "This is Beth, my sister," she introduced them. "This is Sara. She is in the book club with me."

"You have a book club?" Beth asked.

"Yes we do," Sara answered sweetly.

Beth sat down in a chair and said, "Don't mind me."

Anna was a little disappointed that Beth didn't seem very interested in her job, but she started the usual conversation she had with Sara. They talked for a little while about Greek mythology, but Sara had to leave after a while to go to her extra-curricular writing class.

Once she was gone Beth asked, "How old is she?"

"Who Sara?" Anna asked. "I think she is seven."

"So on the last Friday of every month you come here and talk with a little girl who is almost ten years younger than you about Greek mythology?" Beth asked.

"Well you could put it like that if you wanted, but what's wrong?"

"Nothing, nothing," Beth grinned.

Eighteen

Their life in town became more and more normal and even though it was hard to forget all that had happened to them in the last four years, it was not on their mind as much as it used to be. Of course they never forgot their parents or their treacherous aunt. How could they?

They were always on the lookout for strange things in the newspaper or gossip around the town and they soon noticed that people kept disappearing after they went for a job interview. The job interviews were all at places that had no connection. First Ellina Roberts vanished after she had a job interview for a job at a bookstore. Then Christopher Lacey disappeared after he was offered a job at a hospital. He was last seen walking to a bus stop after the interview. There were many more after this. The stories seemed to have no connection with their aunt, but Anna checked every newspaper, just in case. One day she came upon an important article. It read,

July Melvins, the CEO of our neighborhood film company, claims to have no idea where her latest employee went. According to her, Elizabeth Jones had accepted the job and walked out of the office building around 6:00 pm. July Melvins saw her walk all the way down the street and out of sight. She claimed to know nothing more.

It showed a picture of a young woman and their aunt, July Melvins. Both girls had no idea what July was doing. According to the rest of the article their aunt was the head of a film company. The article said nothing about that being illegal. Anna and Beth had already decided that they couldn't tell the police since their aunt captured their parents. Since neither of them could understand why their aunt had appeared in the newspaper, it seemed like there was nothing they could do.

When their attempt to discover what their aunt was doing seemed hopeless, Anna had an idea. She decided to ask Sara. "I know, I know, not many people would ask eight year olds about things like this, but if anybody could help it would be Sara," Anna explained when she had seen the skeptical look on Beth's face. So on the last Friday of that month, Anna was sitting at the librarian's desk patiently waiting and reading a book. Meanwhile Beth was walking around nervously and fiddling with books. She would flip them open and after reading the first page, decide they were too boring, too simple, too challenging, too long, or too short.

"Will you stop it?" Anna asked exasperatedly. "It's not like we're going to set off a bomb." When Sara finally came, they all sat down. Beth was still fiddling, but stopped when Anna gave her a look.

Anna presented their situation to Sara, but she didn't want to tell the whole truth, "I was thinking about a story I might write someday. Where there are two twins like us," she gestured to Beth and herself, "who has an evil aunt. Their aunt is doing something illegal, but they don't know what it is. One day their aunt shows up in the newspaper when a woman disappears after she was interviewed by their aunt. I'm kind of stuck at that point. Do you know what you would put in there?" Anna felt kind of bad about lying to Sara, but she and Beth couldn't get any other people tangled up in their problems.

"Well," Sara said, obviously thinking hard, "does anybody work for their aunt?"

"Yes," Beth answered for Anna.

"Then I would think that she was hiring people to work for her and that's why they disappeared after the job interview, because they would have to live in secret and never tell anybody about the job."

Beth's mouth dropped open in surprise. Anna said, "Thanks for the idea, Sara." Sara stood up and walked over to her parents where they were waiting patiently with Sara's little sister, Jessica.

"So what are we going to do now?" Beth asked Anna expectantly.

"Nothing," Anna replied. "If we do, July might find out that Sara helped us and we have to protect her from that."

"So we're just going to let our own parents live alone somewhere in the world so we can protect a little girl?" Beth asked.

"Yes," Anna answered, "that is exactly what we are going to do." She left the library with those words hanging the air.

Nineteen

One Thursday Anna was sitting at the librarian's desk checking in books. It had been a very quiet day and not one person had come to check out any books, so Anna was surprised when she heard the bell on the door announce a visitor. Sara walked up to the desk. "Hey Sara," Anna greeted her, "you know it's not Friday right?"

"Yes," Sara answered, "but this is important."

"Okay."

"So remember when I interviewed you about your family members for school?"

Anna did remember, it had been a painful subject for herself and Beth, but they tried their best to answer the questions. "Yes."

"Well I heard my parents talking about someone called July Melvins and how she was in the newspaper. I remembered that your mother's maiden name was Melvins and you had asked me about the story you were writing. I kind of put two and two together and I figured it out. Don't be mad at me," she finished up quickly.

Anna looked at her. Sara's eyes were big and pleading. She looked at Anna with uncertainty like she expected to get yelled at. Anna gave in to her big eyes, "Of course I'm not mad at you. Beth and I just wanted to keep you safe."

Sara looked confused. "Why didn't you just tell me? I could've helped."

"You did help. You gave us an idea about what our aunt might be doing," Anna explained softly.

"Which you haven't investigated by the looks of it. Otherwise you wouldn't still be sitting in this library checking books out!" Sara said furiously. "You could have already found you parents and had your aunt in jail if you didn't stop to worry about me."

Anna was surprised by Sara's fierce behavior. She was usually patient. Sara picked up her bag and got up. When she reached the door and had her hand on the door knob she turned around and said, "Would you really give up your parents for me?"

Twenty

Sara didn't come to book club the next day, or the time after that. She was probably trying to convince Anna to help her parents with this boycott. It was not getting Anna any closer to being convinced and it was definitely not lifting her spirits.

Beth was also ignoring Anna. Living on such a small island together made it hard, but Beth went out of her way to avoid Anna when she was picking berries, fishing, or collecting water. She even went back to the lean-to they had created for her when they first had come to the island. Anna recognized what Beth was doing. It was what Anna did to Beth when they had first come to the island. Anna had shut her out and stayed closed up and concealed. That's what Beth was doing now. It felt cold and lonely. Anna wanted to rush over to Beth and tell her how sorry she was, but she couldn't do that. She had to protect Sara and her family.

Sometimes Anna wondered why she was putting Sara and her family before her own family. It was like all the superhero movies. The superheroes couldn't let the innocent bystanders get hurt. The only problem with this comparison was Anna didn't consider herself a superhero.

Twenty-One

After a few more book clubs without Sara, Anna decided to not come to the mainland at all. She refused when Beth showed up at the cave to take her to the mainland. She might have imagined it, but she thought she saw a little glimmer of sympathy in Beth's eyes as she turned to go to the boat. Anna sat on the cave floor all alone for one week. In a way she was relieved, Beth wasn't there to turn her back on her every time she tried to catch her eye. Anna could walk freely to the berry bush and back without having to worry about Beth walking the long way around the island to avoid her. But she was also sad, she was all alone except for Sheila. She didn't have the reassuring presence of her twin anymore.

Anna spent most of the week in her cave with Sheila. It snowed, but she didn't even go outside. Sheila had other ideas. Once the snow started falling, she bounded outside and immediately sunk deep into the snow. It reminded Anna of the time when it had snowed. Sheila and Mr. Fluffy Pants had sunk so deep in the snow the sisters had to pull them out. That was before they knew they were related. They were so naive then. They had escaped and they were free from all the worries of the world. It was before they knew about their aunt or their parents.

Anna wished she and Beth could go back to that forest and live like they had before. But they couldn't do that now, they knew too much to turn around.

Anna started thinking about the orphanage. She hadn't even thought about her old friends for years. She missed them. Anna just wanted to see a part of her old life, the life before everything bad seemed to happen to her. The life where she was a normal teenager, not a teenager in the middle of some epic soap opera with a long lost twin, an evil aunt and kidnapped parents. She decided that she was going to her old home. Not forever, just for a little bit. Anna needed to get away for a bit, away from Beth, away from Sara, away from her aunt, away from everything.

Anna said nothing to Beth about her plan. She would probably think Anna was being selfish. So Anna silently planned for one month. When the boat was ready and the bags packed, they got in the boat and started towards the mainland. It was awkward and quiet the entire ride. Beth rowed and Anna sat there, staring off into space.

Anna was ecstatic about meeting her friends at the orphanage, but she couldn't show it or Beth might suspect something. She patiently sat in the boat until they got to the mainland. But once they got there she didn't head to the library or their home, she walked back to the train station. The trail was just as it had been the last time she walked it, but this time she didn't have the comforting presence of Beth.

When she finally got to the train station she bought a ticket with some of her money and got on the train. Anna sat down in the seat that she and Beth sat in four years ago. It brought back many memories. She remembered that Beth seemed way too curious for her own good. She asked so many questions and Anna knew what asking questions led to. When you asked too many questions sometimes you would find answers to things you would rather have unanswered. That's how they found out about their parents and that's how Sara figured out their secret. Sara. Anna wished she had made Sara promise that she wouldn't tell because there was nothing that could stop her from telling her parents all about Anna and Beth, the two girls without parents. While part of Anna wished that she had someone who could help her, like Sara's parents, she knew that it would put them in too much danger. *You know things and here you are sitting on a train all safe without anybody trying to kidnap you,* a voice in her head pointed out. *But our aunt promised our parents we would be safe so we are. Sara and her parents were no part of that agreement,* she argued. *Oh, great, now I'm talking with myself. What's next, an imaginary friend?* Anna thought.

Anna couldn't wait for the train to pull up at the station. The ride seemed to take hours and hours while in reality it only took about thirty minutes. When the train finally arrived, the orphanage wasn't far away. Anna could easily run there. She broke into a sprint. When she finally reached the orphanage she caught her breath and knocked on the door. When the door opened someone very familiar was standing behind it. "Hi. I'm home."

Twenty-Two

Lizzie looked so surprised Anna almost laughed. "Did you think you got rid of me?" she asked. Lizzie looked older. She was now sixteen, just one year younger than Anna.

"Um," Lizzie said, "sort of." She led Anna into the orphanage. "Are you looking for Charlene?"

"Yes," Anna said excitedly. "Where is she?"

"She got adopted just a month after you left," Lizzie answered dully. "Everyone else our age got adopted too. Now it's just me and some eight year olds." Anna's heart sunk. She had journeyed all the way here to see her best friend and all she got was a middle school bully.

The trip turned out to be shorter than she thought. Lizzie showed her around the orphanage. Before Anna left she asked Lizzie not to tell Ms. Melvins about her visit in case she was inclined to tell the police. As she walked down the block she thought about Charlene. When she left the orphanage four years ago she had always thought she would come back, but she had never even thought that none of her friends would be there.

Suddenly Anna came up with an idea. She ran back to the orphanage and knocked again. When the door opened she said, "I have a plan." Anna got

Lizzie to ask Ms. Melvins where Charlene was living now.

"Hey!" Anna exclaimed when Lizzie told her the address. "That isn't far from here! I could walk!"

So Anna set off toward the house. The houses became more and more elegant as Anna got closer. When she reached the house number she took a deep breath and knocked. The door opened and behind it stood a very surprised Charlene.

Anna smiled. "Miss me?"

Charlene stared at her for about two minutes and then hugged her. "Yes, yes I did."

After Charlene led Anna into her house she demanded to know everything that happened. Anna knew she could trust Charlene with anything so she told her everything. Once she was done Charlene stared at her and said, "So after you left the orphanage you met your long, lost sister Beth and discovered that your aunt captured your parents. Then you ran away with Beth to an island and came to the mainland on the last week of every month where you work in a library and have a book club with an eight year old."

"Yep," Anna confirmed what Charlene had said, "that pretty much sums it up."

"So when do I get to meet Beth?" Charlene asked excitedly.

"Well," Anna admitted slowly, "she is kind of mad at me right now."

"Why?" Charlene asked. When Anna was done explaining she said, "Oh." Grabbing hold of Anna's arm, she announced, "You're coming with me."

Charlene pulled Anna all the way to the train station and she bought them both tickets. Anna didn't protest all the way to her home, but she knew that Charlene would have no chance convincing either her or Beth to switch sides. They stepped through the door of the apartment and Charlene gasped. She seemed surprised at how good it looked. It wasn't very big, but it definitely was tidy. It had two bedrooms with a queen sized bed in each. The only other rooms were the kitchen, the bathroom and the living room. They had put up a Christmas tree and were planning to stay for Christmas.

"How did you afford all this?" Charlene asked in surprise. "No offense, but I thought you were living in a cave or a lean-to or something."

Anna laughed. "No, that's my other home. I could put a bumper sticker on my car that says 'My other home is a cave'. If I had a car, or if I knew how to drive." Anna frowned. "I really should be getting around to that." Charlene laughed.

Then Beth walked in. She stared at Charlene in surprise. Anna broke the awkward silence, "Um, Beth this is Charlene. Charlene this is Beth."

"Why is she here?" Beth asked bluntly.

"Well she kind of dragged me here from her house about thirty miles from here," Anna answered.

"She dragged you *thirty* miles?" Beth asked in disbelief.

"Well no, she dragged me on a train and then we rode it here," Anna said like it was obvious.

"So *why* did she drag you here?"

"I don't know. Ask her," Anna said even though she knew the answer.

While Anna and Beth were having this discussion Charlene explored the room and tried to pretend that she wasn't there, even though this was hard when the topic of the conversation was her.

When she heard Anna she said, "Yes, please, ask me." Beth turned toward her in a sarcastic air of great curiosity and crossed her arms. Charlene stared at her, surprised at her rudeness. Beth raised her eyebrows in exasperation and Anna motioned for Charlene to continue from behind Beth.

"Well," Charlene said, "I was hoping I could help you two with your argument."

Beth twisted around and stared at Anna who was looking slightly ashamed. "You told her?" she asked. "You seriously told her?"

Anna's face gave away the answer. "That's the whole reason we haven't gone to the police. You didn't want to get Sara in trouble because she helped us and then you go and tell her about it! What happened to let's save everybody by telling nobody?"

Beth stormed like a wild bull out of the apartment. You could practically see the steam coming out of her ears. If it hadn't been such a serious situation Anna probably would have laughed. Instead of showing her distress at the situation she turned toward Charlene and said, "I knew that wouldn't work. Sometimes you won't be able fix everything."

Anna walked out of the apartment, away from the only best friend she had ever had. Charlene still stood in the room wondering how two sisters could ever drift so far apart. Charlene rushed out of the apartment and grabbed Anna by the shoulder. "All you have ever wanted is a family, Anna," she said when Anna had turned around. "You should at least try to keep the only real family you have had in your life." Anna gave Charlene a desperate look and even though she said nothing Charlene could tell what she was trying to say. Anna thought that she couldn't do anything to get her sister back. Charlene's arm slipped off Anna's shoulder as Anna continued walking down the street. Charlene had to do something, her friend was losing hope. So she decided to try something else.

Charlene remembered Anna mentioning where Sara lived, and without a doubt in mind about what she was about to do, she set off. Charlene knocked on the painted wood door of the house. When the door opened a pretty women was standing behind it. "I'm a friend of Anna's," Charlene said confidently. "I would like to see Sara."

"Oh," the lady said, "she's over there." Charlene let herself be led into the house. Sitting at a table doing homework was a young girl, she looked just like Anna had described. When she looked up her eyes sparkled with curiosity.

Charlene quickly sat herself down at the table and said, "I'm Anna's friend."

"Go away," Sara said crossly. "I won't talk to her unless she helps herself."

"No, that's not it. I want her to go to the police too," Charlene explained.

Now Sara was paying attention. "What?" She looked up from her homework for the first time.

"We are going to the police for them," Charlene said slyly.

Sara looked surprised. "You haven't asked them, have you?"

Charlene answered reluctantly, "Well, no."

Sara studied her for a moment. "Okay."

"So this is what we will do." Charlene and Sara sat there for an hour, planning.

Finally, when Sara's mom called her to say it was dinner, Charlene got up. "You can go back to your homework now," she said to Sara as she was leaving.

"Oh, this isn't homework," Sara said.

"Than what is it?" Charlene asked curiously.

"Oh I just like doing math for fun sometimes," Sara answered as she took the math out.

"Bye then," Charlene said, but Sara was already trying to figure out the value of x. Once she was out on the sidewalk Charlene remembered how much she hated math when she was Sara's age.

Twenty-Three

Charlene and Sara's plan started the next day. They both were going to walk to the police station at 4:00 pm. Sara wanted to get up at 5:00 am before school to do it, but Charlene argued that the police people might not listen as well in the morning as they would in the afternoon. She also didn't want to get up that early.

Sara could hardly wait to get out of school that day (which was a first). Her first assignment of the day was titled, <u>What I'm going to do during the weekend</u>. Even though Sara knew she probably shouldn't tell anybody about what she and Charlene were planning, she wrote about it because she didn't have much else she was doing over the weekend.

Today after school I'm going to go to the police station with a seventeen year old girl named Charlene to talk to the police. We are going to tell them about our friends Beth and Anna who have an evil aunt. Than they will live happily ever after.

When Sara got the assignment back, she read the note her teacher wrote for her.

Sara we are supposed to be writing <u>non-fiction.</u> Your writing this week is obviously fiction. I would like you to do this over, writing what you will <u>actually</u> be doing this weekend. Additionally you misspelled then when you said, "<u>Than</u> they

will live happily ever after." Your final grade will be a D if
you do not redo this assignment.

She had gotten a D! This was the first time in
her life she had gotten anything lower than a B-. Sara
would have to think of something fast. She couldn't
face her parents with a D. Sara quickly took out
another piece of paper and scribbled away. She
wrote the best, fastest and hopefully neatest that she
could do before school got out. Sara couldn't care
less about what she was writing about as long as it
was actually going to happen to her this weekend.

Sara walked up to the teacher's desk and
placed the piece of paper on her desk. "Thank you
Sara. I hope that this time you wrote nonfiction, not
fiction," Mrs. Johnson said sternly. Sara nodded
quickly and walked back to her desk. She was so
embarrassed she could hardly lift her head the rest of
the school day.

When Sara got home she had to tell her
parents that she was going to help Anna with
something so she needed to leave right away. Of
course they believed her. Why wouldn't they? Sara
never lied to them before and technically she hadn't
lied to them. She was helping Anna even if she
didn't want to be helped.

Sara walked as quickly as she could to the
police station where she would meet Charlene. Sara
got some strange looks while she was walking down
the street. She tried to look serious and older, but it

didn't work very well. She guessed that most people don't usually see eight year olds walking down the street by themselves. Sara walked quickly, she didn't want to be asked by any of the people where her parents were. That happened to her a lot actually, because she often walked down the streets by herself. She liked to have more independence than the average eight year old. Her parents were often reluctant to let her walk around the town by herself, but she convinced them she could take care of herself about two years ago. Most of the people in the town knew about her, but there was always the vacationer or newcomer in the town who would ask her why she was out by herself.

When Sara got to the police station and met Charlene everyone stopped looking at her. She could almost sense they were all thinking, *Oh, okay, she's meeting her sister or something. Now she's safe.* Sara was very good at reading minds, as some people would call it. She wasn't sure how she did it. Sometimes she would just look at someone and tell what they were feeling or thinking. One time her parents hosted a party and she was allowed to attend. Sara had asked her mother why a particular person wasn't enjoying the party. Her mother wasn't sure what Sara was talking about. It was then when Sara realized that not everyone could sense thoughts and feelings like she could.

Suddenly Charlene whisper shouted, "Duck!" She quickly ducked into an alley and Sara followed her, although she had no idea what was happening.

"There," Charlene whisper shouted again, "I see Anna. She must have figured out what we are doing."

"Or she's doing it for us," Sara suggested.

Her idea was met with silence from Charlene. Anna looked directly at them and started walking toward them. She showed no sign of surprise at seeing them. When Anna reached them she said, "Well I see I was right." Sara was quivering with fright. She hadn't expected to be caught. Anna didn't seem very angry at finding them there. She just had the same lost look she had when she left Charlene standing in front of the apartment just the day before.

Anna said in a dull voice, "Now that I caught you, can we just go home?" It seemed as if she didn't care what was going to happen at this point. Sara on the other hand cared very much.

"No, we aren't 'just going to go home'," Sara said. "You have to tell somebody about what is happening. You can't just hope for it to get better and then expect it to actually happen." These were probably the most philosophical words ever spoken by someone of Sara's age and both of the older girls were impressed.

When Sara took a breath to say more, Anna interrupted her, "Fine, fine you can do it."

"Exactly! You can't just... wait what?" Sara continued without realizing that Anna had just agreed.

"I said fine, you can do it. I won't ever get you to back down and I guess it is your choice," Anna sighed it out like it was hard to say.

"Yay!" Sara said. "Let's go!"

"Wait," Charlene stopped Sara with her hand and faced Anna. "Do you really want this?" she asked.

"What?" Sara asked. "We just made up this huge plan to do this. We lied to them and I got a D on this assignment." She held up the paper she had written at school. "So how can you decide that you are on her side? If I have to I will march in there and talk by myself. No matter how many people tell me not to."

At the end of her speech Sara defiantly crossed her arms and sat down on the sidewalk. Both Anna and Charlene knew that Sara wasn't kidding so they went along with the plan. They walked in and explained their predicament to the police officer at the desk. She said she could get a police report filed and they would hear back from them in a day or two, but first she would need to interview Anna, who was the victim of most of July Melvins' crimes.

Anna looked at Sara and Charlene nervously and said, "Okay."

The policewoman led Anna into the room behind the desk, leaving Sara and Charlene in the hallway. She directed Anna to a chair and sat down in the chair on the opposite side of the table. The desk was already set for an interview. It had a piece of paper, pen and recording device. The policewoman turned on the recording device and started asked Anna questions.

"Please tell me the story once again from the time you got the note from the head of the orphanage to the time that you got here."

Anna related the story to her and the recording device, uncomfortably aware of the number of laws she had broken. The policewoman scribbled away on the paper which proved to be rather unnerving later on in the interview.

When Anna finally finished telling the story, she was asked another question, "You say that you left the orphanage because you wanted to find your family, was there any other reason for this?"

Anna squirmed around in her chair. The other reason she left the orphanage made her uncomfortable because it made Ms. Melvins sound bad, but she told the policewoman anyway, "I also left because I felt like I was taking up to much space. There were fifteen other girls in the orphanage and if I left there would be more room, more food and everybody would be more comfortable."

The policewoman replied with yet another question, "So your parents left both you and your sister notes believing that you would meet up in the orphanage?"

"Yes."

The questioning went on for about another half an hour before the policewoman turned off the recording device, got up and led Anna back into the main room. When Sara and Charlene saw her they both stood up and walked over.

"You're back," Sara exclaimed, "We thought that you got lost in another dimension where you had to battle giant hermit crabs!" Anna raised her eyebrow in disbelief. "It's possible," Sara said grumpily. They walked out on to the sidewalk and awkwardly parted ways. Anna reluctantly agreed to let Charlene stay at the apartment as she had the night before. Anna and Charlene walked into the apartment and met Beth.

Beth suspected that something was going on. "Okay. What did you do now?" she asked impatiently.

"Well," Charlene said before Anna could answer, "we did what you wanted."

Beth looked at her and snapped, "I want a lot of things. You'll have to be more specific."

"Well we went to the police," Charlene said like it was no big deal. Beth looked from Anna to Charlene and back again.

"You did what?" she said loudly.

"We went to the police," Charlene repeated herself calmly. Beth stared at her and then Anna. Charlene decided at that point it was best to remove herself from the room. She walked out on to the street and toward the train station. Her work was done here and she had done what she had been doing for her entire life, being a good friend. She bought herself a train ticket and rode back to her house where her parents had been searching for her furiously since she went with Anna to the little town. Charlene knew she was going to get in trouble for her disappearing act, but she had helped Anna and her sister.

Anna and Beth emerged from their apartment, finding that Charlene wasn't there. They guessed that she had left and didn't go searching for her. Anna, Sara and Beth waited by the phone for the next day until they were scheduled to go back to the island. Beth volunteered to stay in case the police called. Anna rode all the way back to the island by herself.

When she got there, she immediately found a spot where she could sit and think. She decided to climb up the hill in the middle of the island. Anna and Beth hardly ever went up there because the hike was long. It was quiet up there though and that's why Anna thought of it as a perfect place to sit and think. Anna brought Sheila with her, even though she slowed her down. Anna climbed up the tallest tree on the hill and found a perfect branch to sit on and watch the sun set over the ocean.

She still wasn't as fond of trees as Beth was, but Anna had grown accustomed to climbing trees. Sheila, on the other hand, loved to be up in the trees. While they sat in the tree watching the sunset Anna was thinking.

Her feelings were conflicted. She hadn't wanted any of her friends to put themselves in danger, but she had also wanted her parents back.

As Anna was pondering if she had done the right thing, something caught her eye. Right in the middle of the hill, the grass looked different than the rest of the grass. It looked fake. Anna dropped down from the tree and walked over to the spot. She looked at the grass, from up in the tree it looked strange, but from down here it looked normal. Anna tested the ground with her foot, she was a bit worried that it was a trap left by hunters to capture animals. The ground seemed sturdy enough so Anna walked out onto the grass, and plummeted straight down.

Twenty-Four

Meanwhile Beth and Sara were sitting in the living room of the sisters' apartment, oblivious to Anna's predicament. Sara's parents had given her permission to stay with Beth for the night and now they were sitting next to the phone with cups of hot chocolate in their hands. They were still waiting for the police to call. They had been waiting since Anna had left for the island. There had been no phone calls since then and eventually Beth had to get Sara to bed. It took a lot of persuading for that to happen, but it did after Beth promised she would wake Sara up if she got a call, even if it was one in the morning.

Beth sat by the phone while Sara slept on the couch. It was hardly after midnight when the phone rang. Beth was awakened from a light sleep by the ringing. She jumped up, grabbed the phone and said tentatively, "Yes?"

The police explained quickly, "July Melvins has been caught stealing DVDs, copying them and selling them."

Beth thanked the police and hung up. She gently woke Sara up and said, "We're going to have an interesting day tomorrow."

The next day Beth and Sara took a police boat to the island to get Anna. They were concerned when they couldn't find her. The boat was still there so she couldn't have left the island that way. The island was searched top to bottom, but there was no sign of her. Sara and Beth had to get back to their interviews. It was their turn.

They didn't like leaving Anna, but they couldn't miss the interviews. Little did they know that Anna was right underneath the island.

Twenty-Five

Back on the mainland Beth was the first to be interviewed. They led her into the room in the back and asked her to sit down. The policewoman sat across from her and began to ask her some questions.

"Please tell me your version of the story."

Beth told her everything that had happened since she had found out that her parents had gone missing.

"You said that you went with Anna because you wanted to find your family, was there any other reason?"

"Yes," Beth admitted. "I also left because I thought that whoever kidnapped my parents would also kidnap me. I was scared."

The policewoman nodded and asked another question, "What will you do when we find your parents and July Melvins is fined or put in jail?"

Beth was surprised by this question. "I will live with Anna and my parents again."

The policewoman questioned her for at least ten minutes before she told Beth that she could go and asked if she would send Sara in. After Sara went in to be interviewed, Beth sat down in the lobby and waited. She didn't have to wait very long, it seemed as if the police decided not to question Sara as extensively as they had questioned Anna and Beth. Sara returned in just a few minutes with the policewoman who asked Beth to come over and speak to her.

"July Melvins has will be paying a fine of $250,000 and will be in jail for five years, because of the copyright infraction and will spend another fifteen years in jail for kidnapping Anna when she was two," the policewoman informed her.

"I'll tell Anna. Why didn't you want Sara to hear this?" Beth asked, looking over to the place that Sara was waiting for her.

"She doesn't seem to understand that this isn't a game and she could be in trouble if July Melvins somehow escapes," the policewoman explained. "I don't want her to start believing she is safe now that July Melvins is in police custody. All the people that work for her are still out there and are probably not very happy with you girls."

Beth crossed her arms. "Sara is a smart girl, she won't let herself get caught."

"If you tell her, you will be putting her in danger."

"You owe a whole lot to that girl. If she hadn't convinced Anna to come here all those filming companies would probably be losing money and people would still be losing jobs. She deserves to know." Beth turned her back on the policewoman and walked to Sara.

When she reached Sara she said, "Sara, July Melvins is going to be in jail for twenty years and will be fined $250,000."

"Yay!" Sara exclaimed and just for a moment Beth doubted what she had done. It seemed like Sara really did think that it was all a game.

Twenty-Six

"I don't know where we are, Sheila," Anna said. They were in a dark tunnel made of dirt. It was obviously underground, but that was about as much as Anna knew. She was talking more for her benefit than for Sheila's. It seemed as if they had been walking hours, but Anna wouldn't know because it was pitch black.

Finally, when Anna was just about to collapse from exhaustion, she saw light. It was very faint, but it kept her going. After a few more minutes of walking the tunnel opened up and Anna was in a place that looked, well it looked fabulous. It was a whole town. There was sunlight shining, but that couldn't be right. They were underground. There was only one thing missing from the town. There were no people. Well, almost no people. There were two people walking toward her. They looked very familiar. Anna saw this every time she looked in a mirror or at Beth. It was obvious, these people were her parents.

Twenty-Seven

Anna asked, "Who are you?" although she already knew.

"I'm Annabeth Mayes and this is John Mayes," Annabeth, no, her mom said. Anna's mother didn't know that they were related!

"Who are you?" her dad asked.

"I'm your daughter's friend." Anna said. She didn't want to tell them yet. Anna couldn't tell why she wanted to keep this a secret, but she did. At least until Beth came.

"Well then I guess that Beth is looking for us," her mom said. "Took her quite a long time." Anna told them the whole story right from the start. She left out the part when she and Beth found out they were twins, but the rest was entirely true.

"Well, then we'll have to wait for Beth to come down and get us," her father concluded after Anna was done. They led her into their house. It was large, much larger than Anna and Beth's apartment. It had many rooms. There was enough space for at least ten people to live in comfortably. Anna and her parents sat awkwardly in the living room for what seemed like hours.

Soon Anna drifted off to sleep on the couch, exhausted from the journey to the village. She dreamed that she was being chased by a monster that she couldn't see. Soon she came upon a cliff and was cornered, Anna turned around to face the monster and saw that it was July Melvins.

Suddenly the front door burst open to reveal Beth and Sara, waking up Anna.

"How did you know this was our house?" Annabeth asked after much hugging.

"Biggest house in the town, it had to be yours," Beth said happily. "Aren't you glad that you found her at last?" She pointed at Anna.

"What are you talking about?" Annabeth asked.

"You haven't told them?" Beth asked, staring at Anna. "That's Anna, my sister."

Twenty-Eight

Everyone stared at Anna for a while and she felt like sinking into the ground and disappearing from everybody's stares.

Sara decided that she should leave and let them work it out without her. She walked down the street to explore. There were many other houses on the street, enough for her entire class at school to live with their families. Ugh, school. Sara wondered if her teacher had told her parents about the D yet. They would probably storm right up to Anna and Beth's apartment and find that she was missing.

Maybe they hadn't even noticed that she was missing yet. With that happy thought Sara turned around and walked back to the house. She suspected that the awkward conversation was over by now and she could enter the house without interrupting anything. Sara was wrong, they were in fact still talking. She was going to have to stay away from the house for a while if she wanted to avoid this conversation.

Then Sara noticed something interesting. There was a mountain not that far from where she was standing. She hadn't noticed it before because she had been facing the other direction. As she got closer to the mountain she could see a cave right at the start of the slope. When she entered the cave she saw that it was dark and dreary. A couple of times

Sara thought she heard a noise and she had to convince herself that she was just being paranoid before she continued on. The tunnel started to slope upward and the climb became steeper and steeper until Sara could see light. Light! If Sara hadn't found the cave then they wouldn't be able to get out. They couldn't go out the way they had come in, because of the drop.

It was funny, they had found the hole the same way Anna had. Sara and Beth were searching the island for Anna and Sara fell right in.

The light was now getting closer. It was almost as if the more excited Sara got, the brighter the light got. She was getting more and more curious about where she was going. Maybe it was Disneyland (this, of course, is every child's dream) or the book store! Finally after ages and ages of walking Sara was at the end of the tunnel and saw that it was most definitely not Disney Land.

Twenty-Nine

Back at the house, the Mayes were starting to notice that Sara was gone. They searched for her in the streets and the other houses. Anna was starting to get scared. What could have happened to her? Anna thought it was all her fault, she had been in charge of Sara. If they couldn't find her what would Anna tell her parents? *Sorry, we lost your daughter in an underground paradise where my long lost parents have been living for four years?* It sounded ridiculous, even if it was true.

Beth ran over just as Anna was about to start hyperventilating. "We found a tunnel in the side of the mountain. Maybe she went in there."

Although Anna was relieved, she grumbled, "Why did she explore a cave without asking first?"

Beth rolled her eyes. "Reminds me of someone I know." Anna glared at her and started running toward the mountain. Beth giggled and followed her with their parents right behind them. Unlike Anna, she wasn't a bit worried about Sara. Beth knew that she could take care of herself. She was very smart for her age.

When they reached the mountain and entered the cave Beth started to feel more uncertain. She wasn't sure if Sara would be able to travel through this tunnel without getting scared. They had been traveling for quite some time when the tunnel finally stopped. The family was very surprised at the sight they saw before them. It wasn't the island they expected it to be. It was a hallway with white walls. The very thing Beth despised. It was just like their aunt's headquarters. Oh. Beth understood with a sinking feeling. Of course. If their aunt had built a jail it would be connected to her headquarters. Before Beth could say anything, they heard the sound of high heels clicking against the concrete floor.

July Melvins stood in front of them before they could even blink. "Well, well, it seems as if you have come looking for your young friend."

"If you... how did you? But that can't...Well, where?" Anna tumbled over her words.

July Melvins laughed a cold, clear laugh. It echoed against the wall and it rang in their ears several seconds after their aunt had closed her mouth.

If they were in another situation Beth would have found her sister's breathlessness hilarious, but this time she defended her sister, "Where have you put her?"

"Oh, you have nothing to worry about, we just placed her in one of our other underground palaces," July responded easily, "and that's where you're going."

"But if you put us in there, then we will just come out the way we came in. It wasn't that hard to find the entrance here. Why would it be hard to find it in another one?" Anna asked after she had regained her speech.

"Hiding something isn't nearly as hard as finding it," July Melvins said simply. The family was led to the place where Sara was being kept. It wasn't that different from the one that the twins' parents were being kept in. The family soon realized why July had been so sure that they wouldn't escape. As soon as they were deposited onto the mountainside, the hole was covered up with dirt.

"But how did she get out of jail?" Beth asked.

"Well, you said she wasn't going to be put in jail until later in the afternoon. Maybe she escaped somehow," Anna said, "but right now I don't really care how she got out of jail, we have to find Sara." She was still very guilty about letting Sara get caught and she wanted to find her immediately to make sure she was okay.

Sara seemed fine when they found her. She was taking supplies from a grocery store and she had chosen a house to pile everything into. It seemed as if she knew that they would be coming. Anna thought she was awfully calm for a person who was just kidnapped, but she decided not to mention it. Sara was probably just trying to appear calm and

Anna didn't want to upset her. Sara had set the house up as if she expected them to live in it for a while.

When Beth asked her about this Sara said, "Well isn't that what we are doing? We told the police and now they can take care of it. Wouldn't it be better to just live here so you don't have to run from your aunt all the time?"

"We are getting out of here!" Beth declared.

Suddenly a voice spoke. It seemed to be coming from everywhere, just like the loud speaker at Sara's school. It said, "Anna Mayes, you will be removed from the village in five minutes. Prepare." The voice was deep and orderly. It was a voice that you would want to obey, because you knew there would be consequences if you didn't.

"Where will they take her?" Beth asked worriedly and grabbed her sister protectively.

"We better do what they say," Anna suggested even though she was shaking. "They have us as captives and there isn't much we can do about it." So when July Melvins came to pick Anna up, nobody protested. It was very quiet that night when they ate dinner, the empty chair where Anna would have sat was obvious to everybody. That night everybody went to sleep thinking of Anna, but all for different reasons.

Thirty

In another underground village Sara was sitting in a house with no idea about what was happening to her friend or the impostor posing as herself that sat at the table with Beth and her parents that night.

Sara was upset at being all alone without her friends and she had been waiting for them to come and rescue her for at least a day. She eventually had to consider the possibility that Anna and her family weren't coming to rescue her for one reason or another. Just as she was about to get up and walk back to the village, Anna was pushed through a hole in the mountainside. "Anna," Sara said as she hugged her, "Where were you?"

"The entire family got captured," Anna answered in a rather robotic voice. "They sent me here and kept everyone else somewhere else."

"Well at least you are here," Sara said excitedly. "If they brought you they might bring the others!" They walked off to collect items and make their house more livable.

Over the next three days, Anna and Sara lived in the house and did chores to get ready for the rest of Anna's family to come, but it seemed as if their efforts would be worth nothing since there was no sign that any of their friends were going to arrive. On the fourth day something strange happened.

When Sara was collecting water from the creek on the mountainside the hole opened up and Anna was shoved through it, again.

"Anna?" Sara asked. "What?" She looked over to where Anna-or who she thought was Anna-was collecting berries.

"Quick," said the new Anna. "We have to go! That isn't me. That's a robot." She pointed at first Anna.

The first Anna who had noticed the commotion came over and said, "What is going on?" Strangely she didn't seem the tiniest bit fazed that she saw herself standing there.

"She said you are a robot. Is it true?" Sara asked.

"Of course it's not true," the first Anna scoffed. "Do you really think that I'm a robot?" It did seem like a ridiculous idea, but one of them had to be a robot or a clone or a ...

"I think that she is the robot," the first Anna said smoothly, "and you're going to have to choose one of us. Who do you think is real?"

Who *did* she think was real? Sara examined their faces and remembered her extraordinary talent for figuring out thoughts and feelings. The first Anna was staring at her defiantly, but the new Anna was looking at Sara as if she depended on her. As if she trusted her. The new Anna looked desperate. Sara knew who the real Anna was. She grabbed her hand and said, "We better get out of here. Something tells me that she won't be too happy that I figured it out."

The real Anna's face broke into a broad grin while the fake Anna positively screamed in fury. Then Anna decided to take Sara's advice and run. They ran down the plain white halls and past surprised employees. Soon they ran into Beth who was breathless.

"Are you real?" she asked suspiciously.

"Yes, we already figured it out," Anna said impatiently. "Now we have to get our parents."

"They're already out. I came back to get you."

They ran out the door which was surprisingly easy to find. The sun shined, the real sun. Not the sun July Melvins had constructed in a laboratory.

They weren't near anywhere that looked like the town at all. Or any part of the town Beth had ever seen before, but there were many parts of the town Beth had stayed away from. She preferred to stay in places she knew more about. Anna on the other hand had explored every alley and street in the town and knew that they actually weren't that far from the police station, where they could ask the police what happened to July. They charged into the police station. Ignoring appalled looks from everyone who had been knocked over, they walked up to the desk.

Anna asked, "Where is July Melvins?"

"Well she…. they took…. Um, she is…" the policeman at the desk stuttered and Anna felt bad for him, but before she could say anything the policewoman who was in charge of July Melvins walked in.

"Yes, she did escape," she admitted.

"Why did you let her escape?" Beth demanded. "She put us in danger!" Beth recounted the story of what happened to them at her aunt's headquarters.

The policewoman put her hand up. "You didn't let me finish. She did escape, but that was only because we let her. We gave her a chance to escape, but only after we put a tracking device on her."

Anna laughed. "Oh, she is good."

The policewoman allowed herself a small smile before returning to the point, "Now did you say the she replaced you with *robots*?"

"Yes she did," Anna explained, "She captured Sara first and made a robot of her. When we came to rescue her they put us with the robot, not her. I figured it out eventually and escaped. I guess Beth and my parents figured it out to. I think that they were going to take us out one by one and replace us with robots, so in the end each one of us would be living with robots of everybody else. The robots would most likely try to keep us from leaving if we found a way out. My question is where did she get all that technology? It's not like we have realistic androids walking around the street."

"Interesting," the policewoman pondered. "My theory is that she took some technology from the nearby extraterrestrial research building."

"You guys have an extraterrestrial research center?" Anna asked.

"Yes, we do," the policewoman confirmed, "and we really don't want the whole world to know about it. I'm only telling you about it because you have already encountered some of the technology."

"Okay," Beth said. "We won't tell anybody."

"I think I have a plan." Anna told them.

Thirty-One

The family was soon standing at the front door of July Melvins' headquarters. They had followed the tracking device's signal all the way there. Beth took a deep breath and knocked on the door. The deep sound echoed down what sounded like a long hallway. The door was opened and behind it stood a surprised July Melvins.

Their aunt soon got over her surprise and gruffly had them taken into the building. Anna smiled and walked in after them. She was still marveling at the brilliance of her plan. The plan was to place a replica of her (made in the extraterrestrial research building) with her family. Her family did not know that they were with a robot, not Anna. They just trusted her plan, even if they knew nothing about it. Then Anna would slip in and call the police using a radio to confirm that they were in the right place. The police would come and boom, July and her team would be arrested and Anna could live happily ever after with her family.

Suddenly Anna heard a sound down the hall. She quickly darted into a room and quietly closed the door behind her. She breathed a sigh of relief before realizing that she had no idea if anyone else was in the room with her. Anna whipped around and saw that she was the only person in the room. The room looked like an observation room. It looked over another room from above. Anna looked down at the room and saw that her parents and July Melvins were standing there. Her mother was standing face to face with her aunt. They were waving their hands around.

Anna pressed a button, hoping that she would be able to hear the conversation somehow. She wasn't disappointed. It seemed as if speakers were all around the room because Anna could hear her family perfectly.

Her aunt was saying, "I can still put her back in the orphanage." She pointed at the fake Anna.

"No you can't! The police are probably coming right this instant!" Sara exclaimed.

The police! Anna had completely forgotten to call them to confirm that this was the right place. She whipped out the walkie-talkie and said, "This is the right place."

There was no reply, but Anna knew they had gotten her message. Claire (the policewoman) had promised that they would be monitoring the walkie-talkie every second until they got her call. Anna turned back to the speaker to hear what was happening. It looked like her aunt was just finishing a big speech, "...and there is nothing you can do to stop me."

"There is a lot we can do to stop you because we won't let you take her!" Beth said and with that Anna's family stood in front of her in protection. Anna realized this was the family she always wanted, because they were willing to protect her no matter what it took. Anna opened a door that led to a balcony overlooking the room.

"Even that won't stop me!" July cackled triumphantly.

"Are you sure?" Anna said as she stepped out of the shadows. "Because I'm not."

"But you're there." July pointed at the Anna robot.

"You made it really obvious that you weren't the one who created that technology." Anna smiled.

"This changes nothing," their aunt said. "I still have the upper hand."

"Really? In all the books I have read the person who has the police on their side usually has the upper hand and trust me I have read a lot of books," Anna said.

"She has!" Beth exclaimed. "I'm pretty sure that's the only thing she does!" Right on cue the police burst into the room.

For Beth the rest of the day was a blur. For years after, all she could remember was thinking that it was ridiculous that Anna had been kept apart from her parents for almost sixteen years because of film copyrights. After everything had been put right, Anna and Beth left the town, but only after promising Sara that they would come and visit. When the family got back to the house, they found that it had fallen into disrepair. It was obvious no one had been there since Beth left four years ago. Cleaning it up took two weeks, but when it was done the house looked perfect.

Every night before they went to bed Anna would tell the story of how they came together at last, just like she had always dreamed of doing.

Acknowledgments

Firstly, I would like to thank my family for all their help and support while I was writing this book. I couldn't have gotten past the second draft without them. Judy, Wayne, Malcolm, Maureen, Shirin, Heather, Darrow, Aria, Jesse, Sherry, Chuck and Lily all helped with this story through inspiration and input. Mom, Dad, and Nathan provided great everyday support and showed me that I could follow my dream and publish this book.

All my friends require a thanks, especially Sara and Jessica, who helped me through everything life decided to throw at me, just like all good friends do.

I would like to thank my sixth grade language arts teacher, Mrs. Gross. Without her this story would have never even existed. My fifth grade teacher, Mrs. Newport, also requires a big thanks!

Last, but not least, a thanks to all the animals that ever stepped into my life and changed it forever, especially Mac, June and Belle who all inspired this book to a great extent. And a special thanks to my cat, Sheila, for sitting right on top of my paper when she decided that I was working too hard.

About the Author

Fiona Fisher started writing *In Plain Sight* for a school project at age eleven, but soon after the project was over it evolved into more. At age twelve, almost a year since the story was started, she published the book. Fiona lives in Redmond, Washington with her mother, father, brother, cat and occasionally a herd of kittens. She spends her time writing, getting distracted from homework and trying to figure out a way to train her cat not to wake her up at 3:00 in the morning.

46180834R00077

Made in the USA
Lexington, KY
25 October 2015